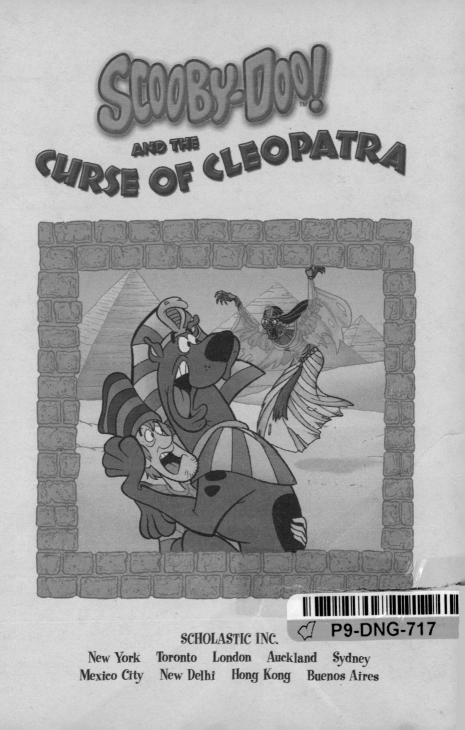

SCOOBY-DOO!
AND THE CURSE OF CLEOPATRA

SCHOLASTIC INC.

New York   Toronto   London   Auckland   Sydney
Mexico City   New Delhi   Hong Kong   Buenos Aires

P9-DNG-717

Copyright © 2005 Hanna-Barbera.

SCOOBY-DOO and all related characters and elements are trademarks of and © Hanna-Barbera.
All rights reserved.

Used under license by Scholastic Inc. Published by Scholastic Inc.

SCHOLASTIC and associated logos are trademarks and/or registered trademarks of Scholastic Inc.

Designed by Michael Massen

0-439-74419-9

12 11 10 9 8 7 6 5 4 3 2 1   5 6 7 8 9 10/0

Printed in the U.S.A.
First printing, December 2005

CHAPTER ONE

In the year 41 BCE, Roman armies invaded ancient Egypt. Cleopatra, the last of the Pharaohs, escaped on her golden barge. Clutching the priceless ruby ankh she wore around her neck, the Egyptian queen watched her city burn from the deck of her boat.

Her kingdom had fallen, yet Cleopatra vowed to protect the treasure of her people. Hundreds of Cleopatra's servants rowed her barge down the Nile River.

They came to the Great Sphinx — a giant monument with the head of a man and the body of a lion. Behind it loomed the three Pyramids of Giza. At this spot, Cleopatra ordered her crew to go ashore and unload the treasure.

Under the light of a full moon, she watched them carry box after box of priceless artwork, jewels, and gold to the base of the Sphinx. She joined them as they carried the treasure down a secret staircase into a hidden chamber. The chamber was the tomb Cleopatra had prepared for herself and the treasure many years earlier.

Cleopatra and her servants carried the treasure through a confusing maze of twisting tunnels and hallways. At the center of the maze they laid a series of deadly traps to protect the fortune. When the last trap was set, they raised a thick wooden gate that allowed hundreds of crocodiles to come into the chamber.

But all of this was just an extra

precaution. Cleopatra already had an army stationed there to protect the treasure — an army of the undead!

A thousand mummy warriors lay in hidden crypts, waiting for the day when they would be called to rise from the dead to defend Egypt's last great fortune.

Cleopatra still had one last thing she needed to do in order to protect her treasure.

"Under the golden crown of Isis I cast my curse," she said in a loud, strong voice, "the Curse of Cleopatra!"

She held tight to the ruby ankh necklace she wore and smiled. Now anyone who dared to enter this tomb would be doomed by the Curse of Cleopatra!

CHAPTER TWO

J inkies!" Velma Dinkley said with a small gasp of surprise. She was hanging high in the air, perched on a rope swing, dangling off the side of the Sphinx. She'd just spotted something red stuck in its side. What could it be?

Reaching out, she pulled the object from the Sphinx. It was crusted over with sand and she used a small brush to clean it. It seemed to be a ruby ankh necklace!

"It's so beautiful! But what's it doing up here?" she wondered out loud.

Velma quickly lowered herself down using the rappelling ropes. She reached the bottom of the Sphinx and walked past many workers and researchers. The place hummed with activity as people busied themselves with different tasks all around the Sphinx.

"Where is Prince Omar?" she asked a man who was unloading a truck. "I have to see him."

The worker pointed up at the Sphinx. Prince Omar, a handsome man in his twenties, was standing atop a wooden platform built around the head of the monument. Prince Omar's wealthy uncle had given him the job of restoring the Sphinx to its original condition. Thousands of years of wind and sand had faded the monument's glory.

Velma had been thrilled when Prince Omar contacted her and asked for her help with the project. She'd spent the last six months there in Egypt helping Prince

Omar and the other workers.

"Omar!" Velma shouted. She held up the ruby ankh to show him what she'd found.

Prince Omar quickly climbed down the side of the Sphinx, leaping from rappelling ropes to platform scaffolding and back again in record time. When he was at the bottom, he hurried to Velma's side to see what she'd found.

"It looks like an ancient necklace," she said.

The expression on Prince Omar's face told Velma that he was very impressed with her discovery. She rubbed the ruby until it shone and then held it up to have a better look.

When she lifted the necklace, its stone glistened in the strong desert sun. Suddenly, the sunlight burst through the ruby center of the ankh and struck the stone tablet that sat at the base of the Sphinx, between its legs.

When the sunbeam hit it, the stone slab began to glow with an eerie light. The light swirled and grew larger. A supernatural wind gathered around the light and created a tunnel of sand and dust.

Velma and Prince Omar huddled together, trying to shield themselves from the sandstorm raging around them.

Then, as suddenly as it began, the swirling storm stopped.

Velma looked down at what the wind had revealed. It had blown away the sand that was covering a staircase leading under the Sphinx. "Jinkies," she murmured in amazement. Turning toward Prince Omar, she saw that he looked just as amazed.

Velma and Prince Omar approached the opening and tiptoed down the stairs. As they descended, it quickly grew dark and they had to turn on their flashlights. Their light beams passed along the walls until Prince Omar's light settled on a mural. The decorated wall was covered in hieroglyphics, ancient Egyptian picture writing, and in the center was a giant portrait of an Egyptian queen.

"Velma, you've found it!" he shouted, awestruck at the sight. "The lost tomb of Cleopatra! It's been hidden for thousands of years!"

Velma swung her light onto the gigantic picture. Her eyes landed on the ruby ankh necklace the queen wore in the portrait. It was the same as the ruby ankh necklace that Velma held in her hands. Had this necklace belonged to Cleopatra? It certainly seemed possible.

CHAPTER THREE

A brightly painted van cut a path across the burning desert. It was the Mystery Machine, carrying Velma's very best friends: Fred Jones, Daphne Blake, Shaggy Rogers, and of course, Scooby-Doo.

Shaggy and Scooby relaxed on the roof, enjoying the sun. Scooby's ears flapped in the breeze, while Shaggy shielded himself with a beach umbrella and poured a glass of lemonade. "Man, Scoob, Egypt is a real hot spot," he chuckled.

Below them, Daphne sat in the passenger seat while Fred drove. They knew

Velma would be surprised and happy to see them. They missed her so much they just had to come visit.

Fred noticed a strange smell coming through the vents. Then a loud bang sounded and white steam began pouring from under the van's hood.

The Mystery Machine slowly rolled to a stop.

Fred climbed out and lifted the hood as Scooby and Shaggy came down to find out what was wrong. "Big trouble, gang," Fred announced. "It looks like our radiator is out of water."

Fred and Daphne noticed a big bird with a wide wingspan circling above them. "That's a hawk!" Fred told Daphne. The hawk circled above them a few times before diving down. In an instant, it swooped between them, and then rose up again, disappearing into the sky.

At almost the same time, a tall figure appeared in the distance. As it came closer, they could tell that it was a bearded man riding a camel. He wore a turban and flowing desert robes. A whole herd of camels trailed along after him. The hawk that they'd just seen was now perched on the man's arm. "*Ahlan wa sahlan!*" the man called to them, waving as he approached. "That means *hello* in Egyptian."

"What's up?" Fred called back to him. "That means *hello* in American."

The man's camel stopped in front of the steaming van and knelt, allowing its rider to climb down to the ground. "I am Amahl Ali Akbar, at your service," he said with a polite bow.

Fred explained that the Mystery

Machine had run out of water. "Do you know where we might find some?" he asked.

"I am sorry, my friend," Amahl replied, "but there is no water here."

"Jeepers! What are we going to do?" Daphne cried.

"Come, join my caravan," Amahl suggested. "We travel toward the Nile River. There you will find what you are looking for."

Two camels towed the Mystery Machine behind them as the gang and Amahl set off across the desert. In a few hours, the unlikely caravan reached the shore of the great river Nile.

Everyone stared at it, completely stunned. Where a flowing river once lay, the earth was now as parched as the desert itself.

The Nile had dried up!

Amahl got off his camel and knelt, clutching a handful of dry dirt. "This is not a good sign," he remarked.

Shaggy nodded. "Like, a good sign would be, *No Diving!*"

"Our journey together has come to an end," Amahl told them as he untied the ropes that had been towing the van. "I must go find water for my camels."

"But how are we supposed to get to the Sphinx?" Fred asked him as the gang climbed down from their camels.

"You have already arrived, my friend," Amahl replied. "It is just over that hill. Big statue . . . pyramids in the back . . . you can't miss it."

Waving good-bye to Amahl, the gang headed off on foot. As soon as they made it to the top of the nearest sand dune, they saw an awe-inspiring sight. From where they stood, the entire work site around the Sphinx was laid out before them.

"What a strange statue," Daphne commented. "It has the head of a man but the body of a lion."

"Good thing we're in the desert, eh, Scoob?" Shaggy joked, turning to his pal. "It must take a lot of sand to fill that kitty's litter box."

Scooby laughed. "Ritter box."

As the gang chuckled together over Shaggy's joke, a video camera on a pole was suddenly thrust in front of them. They jumped back in surprise and came face-to-face with Rock Rivers, the host of the reality TV show *Fear Facers*.

Every week, Rock Rivers took his show to the world's scariest places, looking for proof of the supernatural. It was one of Fred's favorite TV shows.

Daphne didn't watch the show, but

she remembered something she'd seen in the latest issue of *TV Talk* magazine. She'd been reading it on the flight over to Egypt and still had it in her tote bag.

Daphne pulled *TV Talk* out of her bag — a photo of Rock Rivers was on the cover. "What do you make of this, Rock Rivers?" Daphne asked, and read the cover headline out loud: "'Reality show yanked for prank. *Fear Facers* canceled after video of Loch Ness monster exposed as fake!'"

"Okay! So I faked some footage," Rock admitted.

"What are you doing here in Egypt?" Fred asked.

"Yeah," Daphne added. "There's no fear for you to fake here."

"You mean, you don't know about . . . the curse?" Rock Rivers asked.

Scooby jumped into Shaggy's arms,

trembling with fear. "THE CURSE?!" they both cried together, their teeth chattering.

Rock Rivers nodded. "It's all over the Internet. They've discovered a secret chamber under the Sphinx and unleashed some majorly sick mojo."

"L-like, I think my mojo is going to be majorly sick," Shaggy quivered.

"Rine, too," Scooby agreed.

"If the curse is real, I'll get proof of it on tape and then they'll have to put me back on TV," Rock Rivers explained, revealing his plan to them.

Suddenly Scooby's nose began to twitch. *Sniff. Sniff. Sniff.* All at once, he leaped out of Shaggy's arms and raced toward the tent city by the Sphinx.

"What's gotten into Scooby?" Daphne asked as she watched him run off.

"I think he's picked up something on the old nose radar," Shaggy suggested. "Come on!"

"Ret's roh!" Scooby called back to the gang.

CHAPTER FOUR

Velma sat in her tent writing in her journal about all the exciting things that had happened that day. As she wrote, she slowly realized that things were crashing and people were shouting outside. She looked up from her notebook just as a large creature burst into her tent.

She stood up, and the powerful animal lunged into her, knocking her onto the floor. "Scooby!" she cried. "Jinkies! How did you get here?!"

Scooby wet her cheeks with his big, happy, slurpy licks. He'd missed Velma so much!

As she laughed and let him lick her face, Velma saw the rest of the gang enter her tent. "Guys? Wow! What a surprise."

They all told her how much they'd missed her. "Isn't it great?" Daphne said. "The gang's back together again." She noticed the ruby ankh necklace Velma was wearing and went closer for a better look. "What a cute necklace!"

"It's not really mine," Velma told her. "It's an ancient Egyptian symbol. Someday it will go to the museum, where it belongs."

Prince Omar poked his head into Velma's tent and looked around at the gang. "Can it be?" he cried, coming all the way in. "Velma, are these the teenaged sleuths with whom you have enjoyed so many adventures?"

Prince Omar agreed to show them the secret chamber. "We have been besieged by annoying treasure hunters," he said. "But you are different. I will gladly show you."

As they stepped outside Velma's tent, they heard a loud sound filling the air.

Whup! Whup! Whup!

A Blackhawk helicopter appeared in the sky above the sand dunes near the work site. On the ground below, two motorcycles careened over the dune. A huge Hummer raced in behind the motor-cycles.

Ropes suddenly dropped out of the helicopter. The gang watched in worried amazement as two people climbed down the ropes, then dropped to the ground, just above the top of the sand dune. At the same time, a crew of men and women dressed in military-looking desert gear piled out of the Hummer.

What was going on? Were they under attack? If so, who was attacking?

The helicopter landed several feet away from Prince Omar and the gang. A door opened and out stepped a mysterious-looking woman dressed in a wide-brimmed hat and a cape that swirled around her.

The man and woman who had come down from the helicopter joined her as she walked toward the Sphinx. "Ah, nice kitty. Purr for Momma," she said to it, speaking to the huge statue in a silky, self-assured voice.

Velma gasped. "Doctor Amelia VonButch!"

"Amelia Von-*who*?" Fred asked.

"She's an archaeologist and a world-class treasure hunter," Velma replied.

"You mean she's a treasure thief!" Omar said angrily.

Prince Omar strode toward the woman, his face red with rage. He told Amelia VonButch that she had to leave at once, but she laughed at him haughtily. Tossing off her hat and cape, Amelia VonButch began to walk down the stairs into the secret chamber.

"Stop, you can't go down there!" Velma cried.

Amelia VonButch laughed again and waved for her assistants to follow her. "Come, Campbell, Natasha," she commanded them.

Velma watched as they disappeared into the darkness of the secret chamber. Then she turned, looking toward her friends for help. "Come on, gang," she said.

CHAPTER FIVE

By the time the gang caught up to Amelia VonButch, Natasha, and Campbell, the trio had reached the giant mural of Cleopatra. The chamber was glowing with light from the flares Natasha and Campbell had tossed into the giant urns lining the walls.

Amelia VonButch ran her hands along the sides of the mural, examining it. "The tomb itself is sealed," she noted. "Imagine! The crown of Cleopatra waits beyond this door."

Prince Omar came running into the

chamber with a notebook in his hands. "Please wait!" he shouted urgently. "I have just finished figuring out what the hieroglyphics on the mural say! They bear a terrible warning! They tell of a curse that will begin if anyone enters the Secret Tomb of the Pharaohs."

Amelia VonButch looked up at the ancient Egyptian writing. She was able to read it without even looking at Prince Omar's notes. "'The Nile will fall and the desert will rise,'" she read. "'The Army of the Undead will awaken, and all who enter will be turned to stone.'"

"The Nile will fall...," Daphne repeated. The words seemed all too real to her. "We saw the river ourselves," she reminded her friends. "It was completely dry."

"But what does it mean by 'the desert will rise'?" Fred wondered.

"And . . . like . . . awaken the Army of the Undead?" Shaggy added with a deep gulp. "Let's hope they have a snooze button!"

"Ru-huh," Scooby agreed, his knees knocking fearfully.

Amelia VonButch simply laughed at the warning. "Nice try, Cleo," she said, speaking to the mural of Cleopatra. "But we didn't come all this way just to leave empty-handed."

"If there is an undead army down there, our equipment will detect it," said Natasha, Amelia VonButch's helper.

Her other assistant, Campbell, whipped out a long, gleaming machete. "They won't be undead for long," he said with a nasty chuckle.

Prince Omar stepped closer to Amelia VonButch. "In the name of archaeology, let us treat this tomb with respect," he pleaded with her. "I'm sure its secrets can be revealed in time."

Amelia VonButch took a handheld detonator from her tool belt and raised it toward the mural. "I couldn't agree more," she said. "And there's no time like the present." As she spoke, she clicked the button on the detonator she was holding.

KABOOM!

A blast ripped open the doorway just below the mural. Amelia VonButch had placed an explosive device on the wall when she was examining the mural only minutes before.

Prince Omar was enraged. "She's just destroyed two thousand years of history!"

"Don't worry, Omar," Velma told him. "If the curse can't stop her, *we* will!"

Suddenly a strange mist swirled into

the chamber from the outside. It billowed around the columns and statues. Amelia VonButch sent Campbell out to see what was going on. In a few minutes, he returned, looking worried. "You'd better come check this out," he advised his boss.

Everyone ran to the entrance of the tomb and looked outside. The sky had grown dark, and sand was blowing in a massive wave, heading straight for them.

"Jeepers!" Daphne cried, alarmed. "What is that?"

Outside, people ran in all directions, hurrying to escape the wind and sand.

"Sandstorm!" Velma said, realizing what it was.

"'And the desert will rise,'" Omar said, remembering Cleopatra's words. "It is the curse!"

CHAPTER SIX

Everyone ran out of the tomb, but the wind and sand tossed them about. "Unload all the equipment!" Amelia VonButch instructed her helpers.

"Scooby! Shaggy! Where are you?" Daphne called. The blowing sand was so thick that she couldn't see them.

"Like . . . we don't know!" Shaggy called back as he blindly fought the wind. "When we find out, we'll send you a postcard."

Scooby and Shaggy tumbled down the stairwell by accident. They rolled all the way to the base of the mural. They were glad to find Prince Omar standing in front of it, but when they got close enough to touch him, they jumped back in surprise. "Zoinks!" Shaggy screamed. "Prince Omar! He's been turned to stone!"

Turning, they raced toward the entrance of the tomb.

CRASH!

Scooby and Shaggy collided with the rest of the gang. They, too, had fallen down the stairs by mistake and sat in a heap at the bottom of the stairwell. "Guys!" Daphne cried. "What are you doing?"

"Like . . . heading back out into the nice, safe sandstorm," Shaggy replied.

"But why?" Fred asked.

"Just look over there," Shaggy said, pointing to Prince Omar. "Prince Omar and the Rock of Gibraltar could be second cousins!"

They turned to see Amelia VonButch,

Natasha, Campbell, and her masked helpers coming back into the tomb carrying equipment. "It's impossible!" she cried when she saw Prince Omar.

"It's just like the curse promised," Fred said as they walked toward her. "'And all who enter will be turned to stone.'"

"We tried to warn you," Velma added angrily. "Now look what you've done!"

Amelia VonButch looked at the stone Prince Omar for one more second, and then waved for Natasha, Campbell, and her helpers to follow her through the opening she'd blasted in the tomb door.

"Can't you see what's happening here?" Velma asked her. "What's it going to take to stop you?"

"Nothing short of an army," Amelia VonButch answered as she entered the tomb with her two assistants and her crew of helpers.

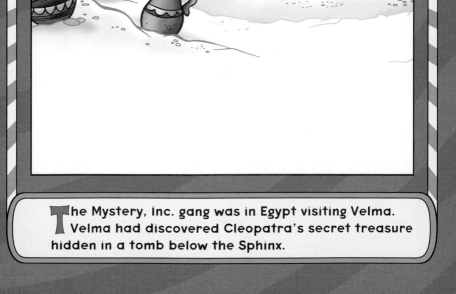

The Mystery, Inc. gang was in Egypt visiting Velma. Velma had discovered Cleopatra's secret treasure hidden in a tomb below the Sphinx.

Velma wasn't the only one interested in Cleopatra's treasure. Dr. Amelia VonButch, a notorious treasure hunter, and her crew dropped in unexpectedly.

Cleopatra's treasure was in a tomb protected by a dangerous curse. But Amelia VonButch didn't care—she blew the tomb open anyway!

Cleopatra's curse came to life! It summoned the Army of the Undead!

Then Velma was turned to stone! Fred vowed that the curse was going down!

Meanwhile, Scooby and Shaggy were having their own adventure! A whirlpool brought them to the Lost City.

Hotep, a magician, and the ruler of the Lost City, threw a big banquet for Scooby and Shaggy.

To fulfill a prophecy, Scooby and Shaggy had to fight a terrifying giant scorpion!

It turned out that the scorpion was just a robot—controlled by Hotep! And Hotep was really just a criminal who tricked the people of the Lost City into letting him rule over them.

cooby and Shaggy snuck back to Cleopatra's crypt and sounded the signal for the soldiers of the Lost City to come on their boat.

melia VonButch escaped to the treasure chamber. When she stole Cleopatra's precious crown, it started an earthquake that flooded the tomb!

Outside the Sphinx, the true identity of Cleopatra was revealed—Velma Dinkley! She dressed up like Cleopatra and dressed the workers up like mummies to frighten away treasure hunters!

Cleopatra's treasure was restored to Egypt, and Amelia VonButch and her crew were captured. All thanks to Mystery, Inc. and "Scooby-Dooby-Doo!"

"Well, gang," said Fred, looking worried. "It looks like we've got another mystery on our hands."

"No, Fred," Velma disagreed. "This time it's just too dangerous."

"Hold on! I must have sand in my ears," Shaggy said, hitting the side of his head and knocking a spray of sand from his ear. "Like, did Velma actually say we're not going to try to solve this mystery?"

"But what about Prince Omar?" Daphne asked. "We can't just leave him like this."

"Come on, Velma. Maybe we can find a way to reverse the curse," Fred said.

Velma looked at the stone statue of Prince Omar. "Okay, guys," she finally agreed.

The gang decided to stick together. They entered the tomb and found themselves on a very high, narrow walkway that wound through a seemingly endless cavern.

Shaggy and Scooby knelt and peered over the side, trying to see the bottom. By the time they gave up, the rest of the gang had gotten far ahead of them. "Hey! Where did everybody go?" Shaggy asked, panicking. "Wait for us!"

Shaggy and Scooby raced forward. They were running so fast that they couldn't stop even when they caught up with the gang. They ran right past them and skidded to a stop ahead of their friends.

"Guys, don't move!" Fred warned them. "You've run into a trap!"

Looking down, Scooby and Shaggy saw tiny cracks forming under their feet. The tiny cracks quickly turned into great big cracks.

"Run, guys!" Fred shouted. Daphne, Velma, and Fred began to run. Ahead of them, Amelia VonButch and her team saw the cracking floor. They also started running.

But Scooby and Shaggy were too scared to run. They stood there, frozen with fear, as the floor crumbled beneath their feet.

The next thing they knew, they were falling . . . down, down, down they tumbled. They leaped from rock to rock, not knowing when they would ever hit the ground — and hoping they never would.

Suddenly, Shaggy spotted an open doorway in the rock wall to his side. Grabbing Scooby, he leaped toward it.

They rolled into a room filled with mummy cases. Shaggy skidded across the floor. When he looked around for Scooby, he didn't see him. Then he heard chomping coming from a mummy case. Upon opening it, he found Scooby eating a sandwich and wearing the headdress of an ancient Egyptian. "Well, how do you like that?" Shaggy joked. "I find King Mutt's tomb — and he's on a lunch break."

"Scooby! Shaggy!" It was Daphne's voice calling down to them.

They walked to the doorway and saw that they were now separated from their friends by a vast opening where the floor had once been.

"Stay there," Fred instructed them.

"So much for sticking together," Shaggy said to Scooby as they gazed across the huge chasm.

Scooby and Shaggy turned back and walked through the room of open mummy cases. "Wow! Look at all these creepy coffins," Shaggy said. "And they're all empty. Not that *that's* a bad thing."

"Ruh-huh," Scooby agreed.

Shaggy suddenly stumbled over something. He had landed in a vat, and when he tried to get up, he couldn't. "I'm, like, stuck in some muck," he said with a laugh. It seemed as though he'd fallen into wet cement.

Scooby pulled him out and they continued on through the dimly lit chamber.

"Hey, Scoob, do you know who tucks a mummy into bed at night?" Shaggy asked. "His mummy!"

A loud groan filled the room.

"Okay, I admit it wasn't my best joke," Shaggy said as a hand tapped his shoulder. Thinking Scooby was tapping him, Shaggy turned.

But it wasn't Scooby.

Instead, it was something much scarier. Shaggy and Scooby found themselves face-to-face with three horrifying ancient mummies — soldiers of the Army of the Undead!

CHAPTER SEVEN

Fred, Velma, and Daphne entered the chamber that held the statue of Isis. They could see Amelia VonButch and her team just ahead of them.

All at once, they heard Shaggy and Scooby screaming from the other side of the deep chasm that separated them. "They're in trouble!" Velma cried.

"Guess what?" Fred said, pointing up along the ledge of the chamber. "So are we!" Hundreds of living mummies carrying swords, spears, axes, and shields growled down at them. The mummies were coming from both sides of the chamber. All at once, the mummy warriors began leaping from the ledge, down into the chamber. They attacked Amelia VonButch and her group first. Her assistants fought fiercely, but Amelia VonButch was the toughest of them all. She swung from ropes that she launched from a grappling gun, twirling and kicking the mummies as she bounced from one wall to the other.

"Wow! She's good," Fred commented, watching as she pounded three horrible mummies with a flying spin-kick before twirling back up to the ceiling.

"Look out!" Daphne shouted.

The army of mummies had noticed Fred, Daphne, and Velma and now began to chase them. The gang fled the chamber, running back onto the high walkway as fast as they could.

Checking over her shoulder, Velma saw that the mummies were right behind them. As she turned back, she didn't realize she was making a wrong turn into a secret chamber.

Fred and Daphne kept running, not knowing Velma had turned off. Suddenly they froze as a terrible scream pierced the silence. "It's Velma!" Fred shouted. They ran back to the chamber Velma had entered and went inside to look for her.

"Oh, no!" Daphne gasped.

Velma had been turned to stone, just as Prince Omar had been!

Fred stepped toward the stone Velma and pulled the ruby ankh necklace from her neck. He handed it to Daphne. "You take this."

Daphne wished she knew where Scooby and Shaggy were. Had they also been turned to stone? "Scooby-Doo, where are you?" she called into the darkness.

CHAPTER EIGHT

O n the other side of the chasm, Scooby and Shaggy were also fleeing the mummy army. They ran into a chamber that was full of secret traps.

Sharp blades shot out of the walls. Scooby and Shaggy ducked, dodged, and leaped over them. Fireballs blasted at them from the walls. Crocodiles snapped at their feet.

Scooby and Shaggy ran for a small opening at the far end of the chamber. They slid through it with not a moment to spare just as its door closed.

"Whew!" Shaggy said with a sigh of relief. It looked as if they'd left the traps and the Army of the Undead behind.

But Shaggy soon had a feeling that he was sinking. "Uh-oh!" he told Scooby. "We're in quicksand!"

They sank deeper and deeper. They were up to their necks in quicksand when the mummy army burst into the room. Terrified, Scooby and Shaggy dove under the sand to escape the mummies.

The next thing they knew, they were falling through the sand into a chamber below. Finally they landed in a wide coffin, but their weight caused the coffin to crash through the floor. An instant later, the coffin was speeding through a chute like a toboggan. When it reached the end of the chute, the coffin shot out into the darkness. Scooby and Shaggy were falling . . . down . . . down . . . down . . . into a canyon that had no bottom in sight.

They'd begun to think that they'd never stop falling when they finally splashed into a wildly running river.

Shaggy and Scooby clutched each other in terror as the coffin was tossed around by the current. In fear, they flattened themselves against the sides of the coffin.

The coffin soon floated to an ancient underground city with high buildings that towered above them. Shaggy lifted his head and gazed up at the city — and slowly raised his hands in the air when he saw who was waiting for them at the shoreline.

About one hundred ancient Egyptian warriors stood on the shore. They all pointed their spears at Scooby and Shaggy.

"Ruh?" Scooby asked, peeking up over the side of the coffin. Where were they? What was going on?

When Scooby spoke, the warriors noticed him for the first time. They pulled back their swords, gasping. They seemed to be amazed to see him.

"All hail the great Ascoobis!" a warrior shouted. "He has returned!"

The warriors dropped to their knees. "Ascoobis! Ascoobis!" they chanted.

A tall man in Egyptian robes stepped forward from the crowd. "Silence!" he commanded in a powerful voice. "What is the meaning of this outburst?"

A warrior approached him. "O mighty Hotep, O powerful magician, the pharaoh Ascoobis has returned."

The warrior went on talking to the magician, Hotep. "It is as the prophecy foretold! Our great pharaoh Ascoobis has returned to us along with his lanky manservant, Shaggenkhamen."

"Like, I hate to break it to you guys," Shaggy began to explain, "but we're not really —"

"Enough!" Hotep shouted, interrupting Shaggy. "The prophecy has been fulfilled. We must prepare a great banquet."

Scooby and Shaggy were excited by the word *banquet*. They hadn't eaten in hours! "That's right!" Shaggy said to the warriors. "Like, he's Ascoobis and I'm Shaggenkhamen." If it meant that these crazy ancient warriors were going to feed them, they could think Scooby and Shaggy were anyone they wanted to.

The ancient warriors gave a mighty

cheer and scooped Shaggy and Scooby up onto a golden platform. Still cheering, they carried them into their gleaming, ancient city.

"Like, man, Scoob. It looks like our luck is finally changing," Shaggy said.

"Reah," Scooby agreed as the warriors carried them into a building where a banquet had been spread out.

Scooby and Shaggy had always dreamed of a feast like the one that was in front of them. They chowed down on stacks of pancakes, plates full of corn on the cob, salad, chocolate cake, ice cream — just about every delicious food they could imagine was on the banquet table.

Hotep approached the table. He explained that they were in the Lost City, a city of people who had chosen to live life as it had been during the time of the pharaohs, with no phones, computers, movies, TV, or anything modern. "So, you guys are seriously old school," Shaggy commented as Hotep walked off.

Scooby and Shaggy were enjoying their food so much that they didn't even hear Hotep's insane laughter coming from the hidden chamber behind the wall. As they munched away happily, they had no idea of the evil he was planning.

CHAPTER NINE

Fred and Daphne continued down a dark corridor. "Scooby! Shaggy! Where are you?" Daphne shouted. As they turned a corner, a blinding light hit them in their faces.

"Fear! Show fear!" It was Rock Rivers, and the light was coming from his camera.

"I knew it!" Daphne cried, shielding her face from the light. "You've been behind this all along!"

"No way!" Rock Rivers insisted. "I'm on the real this time. Come on, I'll show you." He led them into a chamber where the floor was lined with thousands of mummy coffins.

"But this doesn't make sense," Daphne said. "These mummies are covered with dust and cobwebs. It's as though they haven't moved for thousands of years, so how could they have been chasing us?"

At the far end of the chamber was a flight of stairs leading up to a pedestal with a beautiful sculpture of a ram's head on it. At the pedestal's base was a stand. A rolled-up scroll lay on it.

Rock Rivers bounded up the steps with Daphne and Fred close behind him and grabbed the scroll. He carefully unrolled the crumbling papyrus to reveal a drawing of the ruby ankh necklace. On both sides of the papyrus were hiero-glyphics. "I'll translate the ancient writing," Fred said, pulling Prince Omar's journal from his back pocket. Using the journal as a guide, he slowly began to translate. "Help . . .the . . . heavy . . . tourist . . . is pinching . . . my puppy."

Daphne didn't think that sounded right. She took the journal from Fred and read it for herself. After a few moments, she was pretty sure she had the correct translation. "How about: 'The necklace is the key to the curse'?" she suggested.

Fred grinned. "That does sound better," he admitted.

Daphne held up the ruby ankh necklace she'd been carrying and studied it. "So this is the key to the curse," she murmured thoughtfully. "What does it mean?"

"It means . . . ," came a voice from across the chamber, "that the necklace is mine!"

It was Amelia VonButch, with her assistants Campbell and Natasha right beside her. "Hand it over," she demanded as she and the others approached, "and nobody gets hurt."

Just then an eerie light began to glow from the statue. Strange mists swirled in front of the light, and slowly a figure appeared within it.

"Jeepers!" Daphne cried. "It's the ghost of Cleopatra!"

Rock Rivers aimed his camera at the tall woman dressed in a long flowing gown and wearing an ancient Egyptian golden burial mask and crown. "Awesome!" he murmured excitedly as she floated above them.

"Leave this place and never return!" Cleopatra's ghost demanded in a haunting, unearthly voice.

Amelia VonButch boldly walked up to the ghost. "Give me your crown and we'll go," she informed her.

Cleopatra's ghost raised her arms. "Now suffer my swarming vengeance!" she shouted, then burst into menacing laughter.

A dark cloud arose from behind the statue. The cloud was buzzing, and the sound grew louder every second.

"Locusts!" Amelia VonButch shouted as the flying insects filled the chamber.

Daphne and Fred ran, with the locusts all around them. Through the dark cloud of insects, they could see Amelia Von-Butch, Natasha, and Campbell racing along in front of them. But where had Rock Rivers gone? They didn't see him anywhere.

Daphne and Fred ran to the staircase and came out of the Sphinx right behind Amelia VonButch and her crew.

The locusts swarmed out of the Sphinx

after them. Desperate to escape, Daphne jumped on a parked motorbike. "Freddie, come on!" she cried.

He jumped on behind her and held on tight to her waist. Together, they zoomed off into the desert. "Where do we go now?" Daphne asked as she steered away from the Sphinx, leaving the locusts in the distance.

"We need to get help for Velma and Prince Omar," Fred replied.

"I'll say!" Daphne agreed. "I just hope Shaggy and Scooby are okay!" She stopped the motorbike by some ancient ruins out in the desert. "How are we ever going to find them?" she wondered, shutting off the engine, which sputtered to a stop.

Turning, Fred saw a village off in the distance. Shaggy and Scooby usually headed for any place that had food, so he suggested to Daphne that they look for them in the village.

In the village, they came to a bazaar where all sorts of items were for sale. Daphne bought a pouch and put the ruby ankh necklace inside it.

Fred searched around for Scooby and Shaggy but didn't see them. He turned back toward Daphne just as a masked ninja swooped down on her from the ceiling and pushed her backward into a pile of barrels.

The warrior swung back up to a high railing. Fred ran to Daphne's side and, looking up at the ninja, he saw a net being fired down at the two of them. As he leaped out of the net's path, he pulled Daphne along as well. Daphne and Fred escaped being caught in the net, but just barely.

A second later, Daphne pulled Fred

away from a second net. "Freddie! Run!" she shouted. Two more ninjas had leaped down from the ceiling and were headed straight for them. Both of them carried wooden poles, and they blocked Fred and Daphne's path.

Fred ducked the swirling pole of the first ninja as Daphne fought off the ninja who had come after her. Suddenly a powerful gas shot from the ninja's pole.

Coughing, Daphne and Fred slumped to the ground.

Just before his eyes closed, Fred saw one of the ninjas grab Daphne's new bag containing the ruby ankh necklace. Another ninja laughed and took off her mask.

It was Amelia VonButch!

When Fred and Daphne came to, they realized that they were staring up at their old friend, Amahl Ali Akbar. In his hands he held Scooby's collar. "My bird Horus brought me this," he told them. "Come! We must find your friends. They are in great danger!"

CHAPTER TEN

Royal trumpets sounded in the Lost City. A grand parade was under way, and Scooby and Shaggy were at the head of it. The citizens and warriors carried them on a golden, covered platform into a huge stadium.

"Ya know, Scoob," Shaggy said, popping a grape into his mouth, "this pharaoh thing is a great gig, except for one small problem."

Scooby knew what Shaggy meant and sighed. "Rooby Snacks," he said.

Shaggy nodded. "Yeah, like, no Scooby

Snacks! How can you build a great civili-
zation and not have any Scooby Snacks?"
He looked around at the gigantic stadium
they'd entered. Their platform was set
down in the middle of the arena. "Hey, do
you think they played baseball in ancient
Egypt?"

"R'oh, boy!" Scooby answered excitedly. "R'I rope so." It seemed that they
were going to have the best seat in the
stadium — right in the middle of the field.

Hotep entered the stadium and spoke
to the crowd. "Loyal subjects of the Lost
City," he said, "you have chosen to follow
me in the ways of ancient times. But now,
as foretold in prophecy, the pharaoh
Ascoobis has returned."

"Ascoobis! Ascoobis! Ascoobis!" the
crowd chanted.

"And now it is time for great Ascoobis

to fulfill the prophecy and sacrifice himself to the all-powerful Spirit of the Sands!"

Shaggy and Scooby looked at each other, alarmed. "What did he just say?" Shaggy asked.

"Rac-rifice?" Scooby asked, swallowing with a gulp.

Horns blared and a door in the side of the arena slid open. From out of the darkness, a very large creature peered at Scooby and Shaggy. The ground of the arena shook as the monster dove underground and burrowed straight for them.

"Za . . . za . . . za . . . zoinks!" Shaggy shouted.

A giant pair of claws shot up from the dirt. Then a third claw shot up. It was a tail! The monster burst from the ground underneath them — it was a huge scorpion!

Scooby and Shaggy ran for it, making laps around the arena with the Scorpion Monster in hot pursuit. "Like, keep running away, Scoob!" Shaggy shouted. "Maybe this thing is on a low-coward diet!"

They scrambled up a tall pillar to escape. They clung to each other at the top, peering down at the terrible monster below them. The Scorpion Monster dashed up a flight of stairs, determined to get at Shaggy and Scooby. It balanced on a ledge near the pillar and reached its snapping claws out for them — but it reached too far! The monster lost its balance, toppled off the ledge, and crashed in a heap on the floor below. The ground shook, and Shaggy and Scooby were knocked off their pillar onto the floor, too.

As the dust settled, Shaggy and Scooby

looked on in amazement. Gears and springs popped up out of the Scorpion Monster — it wasn't really a living thing! It wasn't even an undead thing or a spirit! It was mechanical, a robot!

The people in the stands gasped.

"No!" Hotep cried, running to the broken creature. He looked up at the questioning eyes of his people. "Do not be alarmed by what you see!" he commanded them. As he spoke, he raised his arms in a sweeping gesture, and the remote control he'd been using to work the robot Scorpion Monster flew out of his long sleeve.

The crowd gasped again.

Suddenly three mounted camels burst through the entrance of the stadium. Amahl Ali Akbar was in the lead on the first camel, followed by Daphne and Fred, each riding a camel of their own.

"This man is not Hotep," Amahl told the crowd. "He is really Armen Granger, a brilliant civil engineer and a wanted criminal!" He explained to them that Armen Granger had been illegally damming the Nile River and routing it to the Lost City so that its people would believe he was a powerful magician.

"I would have gotten away with it, too," Armen Granger shouted, "if it weren't for you meddling phony pharaohs!"

"So was it just dumb luck that Scoob and I happened to fit the prophecy profile?" Shaggy asked Amahl.

"There is no such thing as dumb luck," said Amahl. "I believe fate brought you here for a special purpose."

"Yeah, like . . . to solve this mystery all by ourselves," Shaggy said proudly. He couldn't wait to tell Velma!

The smile faded from his face when he

remembered Velma. Where was she? Fred and Daphne told Shaggy and Scooby what had happened. The gang all looked at one another with worried expressions. Would they be able to reverse the curse? Or would Velma be a stone statue forever?

The crowd carried Armen Granger away as the gang and Amahl slowly made their way to the front steps of the Lost City. They sat on the stairs wondering how they could help Velma. Scooby let out a sad howl that echoed for miles.

Daphne realized for the first time that the bag she'd bought at the marketplace was gone — the bag that held the ruby ankh necklace!

Fred suddenly remembered what he'd seen right before he passed out — Amelia VonButch taking the bag! He and Daphne had been in such a hurry to save Scooby and Shaggy that they'd almost forgotten about it!

"If the necklace is the key to the curse and Amelia has it, then we might be able to turn Velma and Prince Omar back to normal," Shaggy suggested. Shaggy began to cry. "Or else they'll be stone cold forever!" he added through his sobs.

"Hold on, Shag," Fred said. "I think I feel a plan coming on. . . ."

CHAPTER ELEVEN

Okay, you know what you have to do," Fred said to Daphne as he entered the secret staircase of the Great Sphinx along with Shaggy and Scooby. Leaving Daphne behind, the three of them made their way down to the deepest chambers of the tomb.

In one of the chambers, they came to another stone statue, but it wasn't Velma or Prince Omar. "Rock Rivers!" Fred cried, tapping on the statue's arm. "He's solid . . . rock!"

They continued on and soon heard the

sound of scary chanting. Moving quietly and cautiously, they followed the sound to a large chamber filled with giant statues. An underground lake swirled around the statues, and in the lake were crocodiles!

Fred, Scooby, and Shaggy stayed on the stairway leading into the chamber around the lake and ducked down as the mummy army marched into it. Two mummies held Amelia VonButch, who was wearing the ruby ankh necklace. Other mummies held Campbell and Natasha. Amelia VonButch and her assistants struggled as the mummies marched them farther into the chamber.

Fred turned to Scooby and Shaggy. "Okay, guys," he said. "It's time for phase one."

As they'd planned, Scooby and Shaggy

quickly dressed in the mummy costumes they'd brought along. Then, with their knees knocking in fear, they went down into the huge chamber and approached the other mummies.

"Hey, man," Shaggy said to the first mummy he saw. "Like, we're here for the big Cleopatra party."

"Reah, Reopatra!" Scooby agreed.

The mummy groaned and nodded for them to go in. "Like, thanks, man," Shaggy said. He couldn't believe it had been that easy.

He and Scooby did their best stiff-kneed mummy walks to the side of the chamber. They found a ladder and scrambled up onto a balcony to view the scene below. A giant gong hung above the chamber on the other side. The mummies used their spears to push Amelia

VonButch, Campbell, and Natasha up a set of wide steps on either side of the underground lake.

Suddenly, the mummies bowed as the ghost of Cleopatra appeared at the top of the steps. A mummy general appeared at her side. He raised his hand, signaling other mummies to bring in two large coffins. They tossed Natasha into one coffin and Campbell into the other.

Cleopatra's ghost raised her hand and shot bolts of lightning into each coffin. When the coffin doors were opened, Natasha and Campbell had been turned to stone.

For the first time, Amelia VonButch seemed scared. "Please let me go," she begged the ghost of Cleopatra. "I'll never steal another treasure again!"

"You have come far to behold my golden

beauty!" Cleopatra's ghost shrieked. As she spoke, her beautiful gold mask cracked open. An old crone with hollowed eyes and jagged teeth was revealed in its place.

Amelia VonButch shook with terror. "Please!" she pleaded. "I'll do whatever you say!"

"It's too late for that!" the monstrous Cleopatra shrieked.

Scooby and Shaggy remembered what they were supposed to do next. Scooby unfurled his mummy wrap and used it as a rope. He made it into a lasso and tossed the loop out over the chamber. It caught on a pillar across the way.

Shaggy held on to Scooby, and together they leaped out over the edge of the balcony.

G-O-O-O-N-N-G!

The chamber shook with the sound as Scooby and Shaggy smashed into the gong. Slowly they slid to the ground in a heap.

The room still rang with the deafening clang of the gong as Daphne stepped out of the shadows and strode into the center of the chamber. She was dressed exactly like the young, beautiful Cleopatra, complete with a black wig and golden headdress.

All eyes turned to her. "Two Cleopatras?" Amelia VonButch shouted in amazement.

No sooner was Daphne in the center of the chamber than a huge barge sailed into the underground lake. Fred stood at the front of the boat, dressed as an ancient warrior. Other warriors appeared on deck and threw down planks.

They were the warriors from the Lost City who had agreed to help Fred battle the Army of the Undead.

In minutes, they were running down the planks fighting the mummies.

The fighting was fierce. In the confusion, Amelia VonButch managed to cut the ropes that tied her hands. Daphne saw her run from the chamber. She waved for Fred, Scooby, and Shaggy to follow her as she raced out of the chamber in pursuit.

They chased Amelia down long hallways and caught up with her inside Cleopatra's secret tomb. They saw her approach a bust of Cleopatra and lift its golden crown from the statue's head.

The gang stepped back. The frightening crone of Cleopatra had burst in from the other side of the chamber, shrieking at Amelia VonButch. Then it whirled around and stared at the gang standing in the entranceway. "Leave the chamber or be doomed!" it screamed at them.

Scooby jumped into Shaggy's arms, terrified. "Zoinks!" Shaggy shouted.

While the hideous Cleopatra was distracted, Amelia VonButch grabbed the crown and ran from the chamber, clutching the crown.

"Nooooo!" the Cleopatra crone shrieked. Her awful voice seemed to make the entire chamber shake. Walls crumbled all around them as the underground lake flooded in. The gang ran as the wall of water rushed behind them. Amelia VonButch was just a few feet ahead of them, but before long they would all be washed away by the wave.

Amelia VonButch used her grappling

gun to shoot a hook into a wall beside them. With a quick swing, she climbed the rope, still clutching the crown in her hand.

The flooding and destruction had released the rest of Cleopatra's treasure from its hiding place. Just in time, the barge that Cleopatra had sailed on two thousand years ago was washed out of the chamber. The gang jumped aboard as the water overtook them.

Unseen by the gang, the Cleopatra crone jumped in with them as the boat was carried away by the powerful current.

CHAPTER TWELVE

Amelia VonButch raced out of the Sphinx. She laughed in triumph and placed Cleopatra's crown on her head.

It was only there for a second before Horus, Amahl Ali Akbar's hawk, swooped down and grabbed it off her head.

As soon as the bird was out of her reach, Amahl rode up, leading three camels. On his signal, the camels pulled ropes that worked some pulleys on a scaffold nearby. The pulleys dropped a rug over Amelia VonButch and rolled her up in it.

Trapped in the rug, she swung helplessly in the air. "Let me down!" she demanded furiously. "The crown is rightfully mine!"

"You speak too quickly," Amahl Ali Akbar told her.

They both turned to see a wave of water spilling out from the secret stairway below the Sphinx. Cleopatra's hidden treasure floated out on the current, splashing into the dry bed of the Nile River.

The gang in their barge washed out of the Sphinx along with the treasure. They zoomed along the top of the wave that poured into the Nile, until they washed ashore on a nearby riverbank. It was only then that they noticed the ugly Cleopatra who had jumped in along with them. "It's Cleopatra! Look out!" Daphne warned her friends.

Scooby sniffed the air, then jumped across the barge and began to lick the scary Cleopatra happily. He licked so hard that its horrible face soon lifted right off!

"Velma!" cried Daphne, Fred, and Shaggy.

Velma's eyes had been closed, but they slowly opened as Scooby kept licking her. She laughed and hugged him.

"Velma!" someone shouted from above. They turned and saw a mummy general. It was the same mummy that had stood beside the hag Cleopatra back in the tomb. The mummy general lifted off his mask. It was Prince Omar! "We did it, Velma! We did it!" he shouted down to her.

A bird called from the sky. Looking up, they saw Horus circling, still clutching the crown. Swooping low, he dropped it into Prince Omar's arms.

"That was great, but can we do it again?" Rock Rivers hurried up to them, aiming his camera. "I'd like to film it from another angle."

"Like, I don't get it," Shaggy said. "Is the curse real or not?"

Prince Omar explained that when Velma uncovered the ruby ankh necklace, they became worried about looters showing up to steal the rest of the treasure. To scare them off, Prince Omar and his workers pretended to be the Army of the Undead. Velma took on the roles of both Cleopatras, the beautiful one and the monstrous one.

"Then you used quick-drying cement to make statues of yourselves," Shaggy added, remembering the bucket of cement he'd fallen into. "That way you convinced us that the curse was real."

"Right," Prince Omar said. "Natasha

and Campbell are okay, too. We released them as soon as their statues were made. They're probably around here somewhere."

"I added a few touches of my own," Velma said, "like the locusts. I learned to breed them last year in science class. Who knew it would come in so handy?"

"And I was in on it, too. I filmed the whole thing," said Rock Rivers.

"The only thing we didn't plan for was your surprise visit," Prince Omar said.

"But we could have helped you," Fred told him, looking a little hurt that the rest of the gang hadn't been included in the plan.

"It's like I said earlier," Velma explained. "It was too dangerous, and I didn't want any of you to get hurt. I never imagined you'd bring an army of your own back to the tomb to rescue me!"

Daphne laughed. "We have the citizens of the Lost City to thank for that!" As she spoke, the citizens began coming to the shore and cheering.

"But it was really Scooby and Shaggy who were the bravest of all," Fred said. "They insisted that we keep looking for you."

Velma wrapped them all in a hug. "You guys are the best friends ever!"

"And now Cleopatra's final wish has been granted," added Prince Omar. He pointed to the treasures that floated down the river. "The riches of ancient Egypt have been returned to the Nile."

"Rooby-rooby-roo!" Scooby cheered.